THE YEAR OF THE FIRE

by

Lou Hooker

Lou Hooker

Illustrations by

Kristi Visser

Copyright 2004

Lou Hooker

Library of Congress Control Number: 2004093170

ISBN 0-9755106-0-6

Additional copies of this book are available by contacting:

Lou Hooker
6900 Chamberlain
Fremont, MI 49412

Printed in the U.S.A.

ACKNOWLEDGEMENTS

Thank you to my wife, Verla, who gave of her endless time and computer abilities to make this book possible. I am grateful to my children: Becky, who edited and urged me to write of my childhood days; Rod, for his constant encouragement; and Carrie, for her help in designing the cover.

Presented to:

Southwest Chicago
Christian School

by

T.J. DECKER

for his 11th birthday

OCTOBER 24, 2006

CONTENTS

Chapter

1

Easter Disaster

Many years ago in the spring of 1941, five year old Louie lived in a big, white farm house near the small village of Reeman, Michigan. His dad owned eighty acres of flat farm land on two sides of a dusty road. They were a family of eight. Louie lived in the big, white farm house with his dad and mum, two sisters, and three brothers. One sister and two brothers were older, one sister and one brother were younger than Louie.

Spring had come early that year. The snow had melted and the brown grass was already showing little blades of green. It was Good Friday.

After breakfast that morning, Dad said, "Boys, we should rake the lawn and pick up the sticks today." Dad was always tidy with the lawn and liked to get this chore finished early. Louie enjoyed this type of work and was eager to help.

Marve, Harley, and Louie went outside. Marve, Louie's oldest brother, was ten. Harley was seven. Marve found the wheelbarrow sitting in front of the car in the shed. Harley got some rakes and soon the boys were at work. Louie dragged his little red wagon from the back of the milk house. This was so much fun for him. He felt proud that he could help his older brothers clean up the lawn.

Louie soon found a spot under the big willow tree where a mouse had tunneled under a snow bank during the winter. The mouse had built a small nest of grass when the snow bank was high. Louie poked at the nest. Out popped a mother mouse. The mouse ran toward the shed and escaped before Peppy, the family's fox terrier dog, could catch it. Then Louie poked some more and heard a tiny squeak. He looked more closely and right before his eyes were six, tiny, pink mice. They were not more than two days old. By that time Peppy was right there. Peppy didn't like mice. In fact, Peppy killed mice. He quickly bit the tiny mice and killed them. Louie picked up the little, dead mice and brought them to the barn. He fed them to the cats.

Soon Louie had his little, red wagon full of sticks and dead grass. He pulled the wagon load of sticks and grass to the place where they planned to burn them. It was near the garden; past the clothesline where Mum hung up the clothes to dry. Louie didn't know that it was at this spot his life would change completely the next day. It would never be the same.

The boys spent most of the day raking leaves, picking up branches and hauling them to the spot for burning.

Dad was out in the field to the west plowing with the horses, Dick and Don. In the late afternoon, Dad came in from the field and said to the boys, "Wouldn't it be fun to have a hot dog roast out by the garden tonight?" The boys happily agreed.

After chores, Dad took a match and lit the pile of grass and sticks that the boys had prepared. Soon Mum and Virginia, Louie's older sister, brought the food for the picnic out to the bonfire. They brought hot dogs with all the fixens, and homemade bread, all sliced ready to eat. There were dill pickles that Mum had canned the summer before. She had also cooked a big pot of baked beans. For dessert she had two quarts of canned sweet cherries with the pits still in them. All this food was placed on a card table a short distance from the bonfire.

Harley had saved some larger sticks from the fire. He whittled a sharp point on the end of several sticks with his pocket knife. Louie had a little jackknife in his pocket, and he fixed up a stick too.

After Dad asked the blessing, Marve and Harley grabbed sticks and put two hot dogs on each stick for roasting. Louie could only get one hot dog on his little stick. They all crept close to the fire and roasted their hot dogs.

Soon Mum warned, "Louie, don't get so close to the fire!" Shortly, Louie's hot dog was black, but he ate it and thought it tasted delicious anyway.

The Hooker family ate quickly that evening as usual, but there was plenty for everyone. At dessert time, Marve said, "Let's see who can spit the sweet cherry pits into the fire from the farthest distance." All the kids thought it was a great idea, but Mum sort of frowned. Anyway, the kids all tried it. Louie had to stand very close to make his pits reach the fire. Marve won the contest.

Louie enjoyed everything about the picnic. He didn't know that tomorrow this wonderful fun would end and disaster would strike.

After the hot dog roast, Dad and the kids went to church for a Good Friday service. Mum stayed home with Corrine, the eight month old baby of the family.

The next morning, Louie woke up without being called for breakfast. He jumped out of bed and ran to the hallway upstairs. He looked out the south window at the top of the stairs. He looked past the garden to where the bonfire had been the night before. He saw a tiny curl of smoke sweep upward from the ashes of the fire. Louie thought to himself, "I wonder if I can get that fire burning better after breakfast?" He hurried downstairs and got dressed right away.

After breakfast, Mum told Virginia to watch Corrine while she fed the pullets. Pullets are young chickens that are not yet old enough to lay eggs.

Louie hurried to the back hallway and put on his long sheepskin coat that reached his knees. Near the back door he found a rake that was left there from the night before. He hustled out past the apple trees, went under the clotheslines and out to the bonfire ashes.

Louie raked the ashes carefully. No flames appeared. He picked up some small branches that were near him on the ground and placed them on the ashes. Then he raked the ashes again. Still, no flames.

Mum was throwing corn on the ground near the chicken coop for the pullets. She glanced toward the garden and saw Louie playing with the fire.

She yelled, "Louie, get away from the fire. I don't like you playing with fire."

Louie heard her, but he didn't do as she said. He disobeyed and kept playing with the fire. Those ashes would not burn; there were no flames, just smoke. Louie got on his knees and blew on the ashes. A tiny flame appeared. Louie blew some more and the flame became larger. The flames reached his sheepskin coat and started it on fire.

Louie could feel the heat from the flames on the back of his legs. He thought, "Oh, no, what can I do? I better run." Louie didn't know the three rules for such a disaster: Stop-Drop-Roll. He ran screaming toward the big, white house. The wind only fanned the flames and made them burn on his coat and pants faster. He screamed for help. His legs were burning. Mum heard him screeching, but she often heard Louie scream as he played, and thought nothing of it. Louie ran faster, under the apple trees, toward the back door of the house. He tripped on a mound in the grass just before reaching the door. He got up and burst through the door into the kitchen. The flames were leaping from his pants on the back of his legs to his back.

Virginia met him at the door. She was holding the baby, Corrine. Virginia quickly placed Corrine on the kitchen table. She grabbed a dish towel from the rack and swatted at the flames. Corrine began coughing and choking from all the smoke. She began crying. After Virginia had the flames smothered, she ran to the door and called for Mum and Dad.

They came rushing to the house. Dad quickly grabbed a blanket and wrapped Louie in it. Dad took Louie in his strong, farmer arms and walked quickly toward the door. He yelled to Mum, "Let's take him to the hospital. Hurry!"

Mum and Dad rushed out the door with Louie. Mum opened the front door of the car and sat in the passenger side of the front seat. Dad carefully placed Louie on Mum's lap. Dad started the car and sped swiftly out the driveway toward the hospital in Fremont. Dad drove the car as fast as it would go. Louie was whimpering. His finger was hurting and he said to Mum, "I burnt my finger!"

Mum answered quietly, "Yes, I know, the doctor will fix it when we get to the hospital."

Louie was in shock and could not feel the huge burns on his legs. They were numb and had no feeling.

When they arrived at the hospital, Dr. Gerlings examined Louie. His burned pants were stuck to the back of his legs. The back of both of his legs were charred black. Each leg had large burns that reached from his knees to his butt.

Would Louie live? Were the burns too serious for healing? Would he ever see the big, white house on the Hooker farm again?

These were questions that Dr. Gerlings could not answer. He said the first two weeks were very critical.

Louie was placed in a private room. The nurses watched him closely. They checked his pulse and took his blood pressure often.

Dad stayed in the hospital that night with Louie. Mum came after Sunday School the next day. It was Easter Sunday.

It was a sad Easter Sunday for Louie and his family.

That Sunday at the hospital, Louie was restless and didn't know what was happening around him. In the afternoon, he screamed, "There are spiders all over me, Mum, kill them for me!" Louie's feverish mind was fooling him. He was hallucinating.

Mum quieted him down. She whispered quietly, "It's all right, Louie, there aren't spiders," as she rubbed the side of his face. Mum's soft words seemed to quiet him.

That entire week, Louie had weird imaginations and dreams. On Wednesday, he started to feel the pain from the huge burns on the back of his legs. Dr. Gerlings said they were third degree burns over both legs. Third degree burns are the most serious burns.

Dad and Mum took turns staying with Louie at the hospital. They quieted him when he yelled. They prayed with him and encouraged him with comforting words. Louie was so blessed to have such caring parents and family.

On Saturday, one week after he had been burned, Mum asked if she could take Louie home. It was so difficult for Mum and Dad to be at the hospital all the time. There was so much work at home. There were also five other kids at home that needed attention and love.

Dr. Gerlings reluctantly agreed that Louie could go home. But the doctor said, "I will drive out to the farm every day to check on him. He still needs to be watched very closely."

Chapter

2

Bumblebees

Dad carried Louie from the car to the house. He felt tired and sore, but happy chills went up his spine to think, "I'm home again. I did get to see the big, white house again." There was a bed prepared for him in the dining room. Mum and Dad thought by putting Louie in the dining room he wouldn't get bored with loneliness and could be a part of family activities.

Louie noticed an odd shaped object at the foot of the bed where Dad placed him. "What's that?" he asked Dad.

"Grandpa made it. It will keep the blanket from resting on your burns."

Grandpa had nailed together curved pieces of wood to form a tunnel. Louie's burned legs could lie under the tunnel, and blankets could be placed over the tunnel to keep him warm. Grandpa even rigged a place for a light bulb to hang. The light bulb provided heat to keep him warm.

When Louie left the hospital, the doctor warned, "Make sure that he lies on his stomach at all times so his burnt legs are protected from further injury."

The afternoon that Louie came home from the hospital, a lady came to help Mum with work around the house. Mum was planning to hire her to aid in caring for the large family, and a boy with burnt legs who required a lot of attention.

When the lady named Verna arrived, Dad asked her into the dining room to see Louie. He smiled at her as Mum lifted the blankets from the wooden rack to show her his burns. As Louie watched her face, he noticed her eyes flutter. Then she swayed back and forth and slumped to the floor.

"Quick!" Dad shouted, "Get some water, Verna fainted."

Virginia quickly brought some water, and Dad sprinkled some on Verna's face. She was very pale and sat up slowly. Louie stared at her and did not know what to think. Later Dad told Louie that the sight of the burns had made her faint.

The next morning as Louie looked out of the dining room window, he watched a nice car drive into the driveway. It was Dr. Gerlings. When Dr. Gerlings entered the room, Louie offered him a faint smile and then gave a grimacing jerk. The burns hurt so much. The doctor lifted the blankets from him and carefully examined the burns. He told Mum that he would have to cut the charred black skin from the back of Louie's legs with surgical scissors. This would help the burns to heal. Mum had to hold him down while the doctor did this. Louie could not stand the pain.

For that entire week, Dr. Gerlings visited the big, white farm house every day. Each morning Louie watched the road for the doctor. He cried when the doctor turned in the driveway.

The doctor could remove only a small portion of Louie's charred skin each day, because his frail body could stand no more.

On one of the nights during that week, Dad came to Louie's bedside and asked, "Would you like me to tell you a story about when I was a boy?"

Louie was bored from lying in bed all the time. He responded with an enthusiastic, "Yes."

Dad's Story

"One hot day during the summer, my brothers, Joe and Harry, and I decided to go fishing at Spring Creek. We got our fishing poles from the shed and also a pail for the fish we caught. It was the time of year the farmers were cutting hay and putting it in their barns for the livestock to eat during the winter. Butterflies were fluttering beside the road and katydids could be heard in the treetops. The grass along the side of the road was brown from the summer heat, and the weather had been dry for quite some time.

As we walked along, Joe noticed a small bunch of grass in the ditch. He said, 'See that ball of grass; I think it's a bee's nest. Maybe we can get some honey from it.'

We cautiously approached the bunch of grass. Harry poked the nest with his fishing pole. Immediately, we heard a lot of buzzing. Soon several black and yellow bumblebees were flying around us. They circled our heads and surrounded us. They were mad! Suddenly, I felt a sharp pain on my ankle. A bee had stung me.

I reached down to brush the bee away."

"Do the bees bite you with their teeth?" asked Louie.

"No," said Dad, "They have a sharp stinger on the back part of their body that they jab into anything that bothers them."

"I see," responded Louie, "Then what happened?"

"After I reached down to brush the bee away, it crawled up my pant leg. Then it stung me a second time. I tried to squeeze the bee between my pants and my knee. It stung me a third time. By the time I finally pinched the bee dead inside my pants, I had been stung seven times. I decided we had better leave the bees alone and not tease them. The bumblebees had taught me a lesson. I made up my mind that day to never bother a bee's home again.

Joe and Harry continued on down the road and fished in Spring Creek. I went home to Ma, and she put some salve on my stings."

Louie wondered if the stings felt something like his burns.

Then Mum brought Louie a big gray pill. "Here, swallow this with some water," she said gently. "It will make your legs feel better."

The pill eased the pain in Louie's legs, and he soon fell asleep under his tunnel that grandpa had made.

Chapter

3

Black and White Kittens

Two days later when Dr. Gerlings visited the big, white Hooker home, Louie had a high fever. The doctor examined his burns carefully. Then he turned and said to Dad and Mum, "I want you to bring him to the hospital immediately. He needs blood transfusions. He is dehydrated and his body is too weak to fight infection."

They brought Louie to the emergency door at the hospital, and he was quickly wheeled to a private room. That noon Dad and Mum each donated a pint of blood to be used for Louie. In the afternoon, the nurse poked Louie's wrist and started giving him some of the blood donated by Dad.

Soon he began sweating and shaking. The nurses tried to hold him quiet. They could not. He began to thrash and shake wildly. The needle that was inserted in his wrist came out.

Nurse Sophie called Dr. Gerlings. She said to the doctor, "You must come immediately. Louie is shaking violently."

Nurse Sophie gave Louie special attention at all times. Louie felt very close to her, because she was so thoughtful and caring.

When Dr. Gerlings arrived, he said, "Stop the transfusion! The blood donated by his father is giving him a bad reaction."

Gradually, Louie quieted down, but he felt so weak and shaky. That night Nurse Sophie gave him three big pills of different colors. The pills reduced his pain and helped him get a good night's sleep.

The next day the nurses gave Louie another transfusion. This time they used the blood that Mum had donated. This transfusion went much better, and he improved by that afternoon.

Louie's stay in the hospital this time was for another week. Nurse Sophie and the other nurses pampered him. One night Sophie asked, "Louie, would you like some ice cream for your snack tonight?"

Louie responded excitedly, "I sure would." He savored every spoonful as he slowly ate the delicious ice cream.

Another time, Mr. Darner, a neighbor of Grandpa's, brought some trout from his pond to the hospital for Louie. The hospital cook prepared the trout especially for Louie. The trout tasted so good!

These expressions of love aided in Louie's recovery. At the end of the week, Dr. Gerlings gave him permission to return home. It seemed so wonderful once again to see the big, white farm house.

During the month of May, the students of Brookside School prepared a special gift box for Louie. This was the country school where Virginia, Marve, and Harley attended. Each student brought a gift to school. Then they prepared a big box wrapped in bright red, white and blue paper. The gifts were placed in the big box and brought to Louie by some of the students and Mr. Melton, the principal. That night Louie was filled with anticipation. But Mum said, "Louie, you may open only one gift a day." There were thirty gifts. The marvelous gift box lasted a whole month by opening only one gift a day.

Harley helped Louie unwrap the gift of the day. One day Harley said, "Let's wait until the last day with that present." He could tell by its shape that it was a shovel.  Louie agreed, so they waited to unwrap the shovel until the very end.

Louie received several books and a ball. There were games of many different kinds, some candy and nuts. There were also many other toys. He had to wait to use the shovel and the ball, because he couldn't even walk now.

Louie spent many days looking out of the dining room window. The first day of summer came and passed. He saw rows of corn growing just past the barn to the left. He saw windrows of hay lying in the field to the right of the barn ready to be brought by horses and wagon to the haymow. A windrow of hay is where hay has been bunched together in a row in the field.

One day in July, as Louie looked out the window, he saw Les get in the old Ford car with Mum. She was helping Dad and the boys put hay in the barn. Oh how Louie wished he could be outside too, instead of lying on his stomach in bed.

A long rope was tied to the front bumper of the car. The long rope went through a pulley in the barn. The other end of the rope was attached to a big harpoon hay fork. This fork picked up big scoops of hay from the wagon whenever Mum would back the car toward the house.

Suddenly, Louie noticed that Mum stopped the car at a different spot, and Les was sticking his head out of the window. He was pointing at something by the barn. Louie looked in that direction. On the grass in front of the barn, Louie saw some little black and white furry animals scurrying quickly behind a larger animal. Louie lifted himself up with his hands so he could see better. Then he saw Marve and Harley run out of the barn door toward the animals. The little critters and their mom scuttled under a loose board beneath the barn.

When Dad, Mum and the boys came in the house later that afternoon for a lunch break, Louie asked, "What did Les point at from the car?"

Dad answered, "Les thought they were little kittens, but they really were baby skunks and their mother."

Chapter

4

Walking Again

The hot days of July arrived. The first cutting of hay was stored in the barn. Corn was standing tall in the field. Louie watched the swallows build a nest under the porch roof. Mommy and daddy swallows faithfully fed the babies until the day they flew away.

One evening Dad came to Louie's bedside. Dad loved music. He often hummed as he walked around the house or outside. Sometimes Louie heard him singing as he did the chores around the barn and chicken coops.

On this night, Louie said to Dad, "Will you play your harmonica for me?"

"Sure," he answered. Dad fetched the harmonica from the cupboard, and then asked, "What would you like me to play?"

"Twenty Froggies Went to School," said Louie.

Then Dad held the harmonica to his mouth and curled his hands carefully around it. The music gave a soothing feeling to Louie as he watched and listened to Dad play the song. Some of the words went through Louie's mind as Dad played.

Twenty froggies went to school
Down beside the rushing pool.
Twenty little coats of green.
Twenty vests all white and clean.
We must be on time said they.
First we study, then we play.
That is how we keep the rule
When we froggies go to school.

Louie thought of the froggies going to school. He wondered if he would ever be able to go to school. He wondered if he would ever be able to walk, run and jump like other boys and girls. Then Louie closed his eyes as Dad played the harmonica. He slowly drifted off to sleep.

The next morning, Mum asked Louie, "Would you like to go to Fremont Lake and the Mission Festival today?"

Louie eagerly jumped at any suggestion to get out of bed and answered with a wholehearted, "Yes!"

That afternoon the whole family, except Marve and Virginia, piled into the 1937 Ford. Louie, hanging on to Mum's hand, tried to hobble to the car. He stumbled and almost fell in the kitchen. He was too weak and could not walk. Dad carried him to the car and placed him gently on the back seat. He had to sit sort of sideways so he wouldn't sit on his burns. They were not completely healed yet.

Dad drove the car directly behind the benches where the people sat for the Mission program. Louie stayed in the back seat of the car. Harley and Les ran to play with the other kids. Louie watched them run and swing. He heard them yelling and having fun as they played tag and ran around by the lake. He thought, "I wonder if I will be able to do that next year?"

Many people came to the car to see the little boy that had been burned so seriously. Their searching eyes embarrassed him, but it did seem better than lying on his bed at home in the dining room.

Later that week as Louie looked out of the dining room window, he watched Grandpa drive in the yard in his blue car. He saw Grandpa carry some lumber and tools from the trunk of his car to the back porch. Soon Grandpa was at Louie's bedside.

"What are the boards for?" asked Louie.

"I'm going to build some rails on the porch," answered Grandpa. "They will help you hold yourself up as you learn to walk again."

The thought of walking again sent a tingling chill up and down Louie's spine. He asked Grandpa, "Am I really going to try to walk soon?"

"Yes," answered Grandpa, "I think you're about ready to try." Louie got so thrilled over the thought of walking that he wanted to jump out of bed immediately.

"When will you get the rails finished?"

"I hope by tonight," answered Grandpa

"Can I try walking tonight, Grandpa?"

"Not so fast. Maybe you can try tomorrow morning after you've had a good night's sleep."

The thought of learning to walk again for a five year old boy was just too much. Louie had a difficult time getting to sleep that night. He also woke up several times during the night. Each time he thought of the wonderful event of walking again.

Right after breakfast the next morning, Mum put shorts and a shirt on Louie. He leaned on Mum and limped to the back porch. The porch had screens all around, but all along one side were some new rails. The gray rails were just high enough for Louie to grab while he stood up.

Mum brought him next to the rails and told him to grab on tight. Then she let him go. Slowly Louie placed one foot in front of the other. It was painful. His legs were so stiff. Tears came to his eyes, but he was determined to walk. Then he took another step as he held on to the rail tightly with his hands.

Louie was thrilled. He shouted to Mum, "I'm walking!"

Mum smiled and gave him an encouraging hug. He was walking, even if it was ever so slowly. When he arrived at the end of the porch, he had to rest.

That morning Louie walked along the rail many times. He felt as proud as a year old baby just learning to walk.

Within a week, Louie started to let go of the rail sometimes as he walked. Soon he walked the whole length of the porch without hanging on. He thought, "I think I really will run and play outside again like other boys and girls."

25

Chapter

5

Christmas

Christmas was near. Everyone at the Hooker home was cheerful and in good spirits. Mum and Dad spoke in Dutch phrases more often. They wanted to talk about the presents without the kids knowing what they were saying. The kids didn't understand much Dutch. Mum and Dad could understand it, but couldn't speak it very well, just in phrases.

One morning Louie heard them say *kindron*. He knew that stood for children in Dutch. The smile in their eyes also gave it away. He knew they were talking about Christmas presents.

Louie heard Mum and Dad talk about a bad man who lived on the other side of the ocean. His name was Hitler. They said many people were getting killed with big guns. He also heard them talk about a place called Pearl Harbor where many American sailors had died. Airplanes had bombed the American ships in the harbor. Many ships sank with American men on them. This made Louie sad in the days before Christmas in 1941. But, that was happening far away, and he felt safe in the big, white house on the Hooker farm.

On a Saturday morning two weeks before Christmas, Harley and Louie went down in the basement to play. In the furnace room, they found a bag of walnuts. They had picked them up from under a tree on Uncle Garrit's farm shortly after Louie had learned to walk again. Uncle Garrit was an older brother of Dad.

"Hey, Louie," said Harley, "Would you like me to crack you some nuts?" Harley's eyes were laughing. He liked to play tricks on his younger brother. Louie was kind of slow in catching on.

"Yah," Louie answered, "I would like some nuts. Hurry! Crack me some." Louie liked nuts of all kinds.

There was a hammer on a shelf in the corner. Harley grabbed the hammer. He placed one of the hard walnuts on a wooden bench and gave it a whack. Some of the pieces hit Louie in the face. His mouth watered thinking about the good taste of walnut.

"Oh," said Harley, "This walnut doesn't look too good, so I'll eat this one." He chomped down the perfectly good white meat from the first walnut. Louie became impatient and wished Harley would hurry so he could have his turn.

Harley placed another walnut on the bench and gave it a crack with the hammer. It was green and moldy inside.

"This is a good one," teased Harley. Louie picked up the green pieces and put them into his mouth. He chewed them carefully because sometimes pieces of the hard shell were stuck in the meat of the walnut.

Louie then said, "Good! Good!" He really liked the walnut. He chomped it down and asked for more.

The green juices from the moldy walnut dribbled from the edges of his mouth.

From then on, whenever Harley cracked a bad walnut, he would give it to Louie. Louie always responded with, "Good! Good!" Whenever Harley found a good one, he ate it himself. They had a good time together. But Louie sort of wondered why he had a tummy ache later that morning.

The next Monday after school, Dad, Marve, Harley and Louie went to search for a Christmas tree. Dad pulled a big sled behind him, and Marve carried an ax. Harley and Louie walked behind them. It had snowed all day, so walking was difficult. Louie's short, little legs got very tired. His legs were still weak from his burns. He tried to follow behind Dad and the sled. Dad's steps were big, but it still made it easier. Louie chugged along behind taking in big breaths of the cold, crispy air.

They trudged toward "Fisher's Pond." This pond was on some land owned by the Fisher family.

When they arrived at the pond, Louie said, "Look at that little haystack in the middle of the pond."

"That's not a haystack," said Dad, "That's a muskrat house. Muskrats use grass and small sticks to construct their home for winter. Their doorway is underwater. They have passageways that lead to a nest in the center. The house keeps them warm in the cold winter."

"Let's slide across the ice and go close to it," said Louie.

"No!" answered Dad, "The government has a law that says you can't get any closer than twelve feet to a muskrat home. This keeps them safe from humans." This satisfied Louie.

Then they all began to hunt for a Christmas tree.

After some time, Harley yelled, "That tree over there looks nice and tall."

They walked over to the tree and Dad said, "That one will do just fine." Louie smelled pine sap as he stared at the treetop above his head.

Marve called out, "I'm the oldest boy in the family, so I think I should cut it down."

Dad agreed. So Marve gave the trunk of the tree some mighty chops with the ax, and soon it toppled to the ground.

They placed it on the big sled and started for home. Soon Louie's legs were really getting weary. He whimpered to Dad, "May I ride on the sled with the tree? My legs itch and I'm getting tired."

"Okay."

So Louie climbed on the back of the sled. The needles of the tree pricked and scratched, but he thought it sure beat walking.

Harley told Dad that he was getting tired too, but Dad wouldn't let him ride. This made Louie feel special, and he began to tease Harley, "Don't you wish you could ride too?"

When they arrived home, Dad nailed a wooden frame to the bottom of the tree to hold it up straight. They placed the tree in the corner of the "front room."

The Hooker family called the living room that, because it was on the front part of the house toward the road.

The kids were allowed in the "front room" only on special occasions or when the family had company.

Now it was time to decorate the tree. Virginia went to a closet and took down three big boxes with Christmas decorations in them. Then she and Marve wrapped a string of colorful lights around the tree. They also wound one red streamer and one green streamer around the tree.

Then Virginia said, "Harley and Louie, you put the hanging balls near the bottom of the tree. Marve and I will hang them on the top."

Harley hung red and gold ones. Louie placed some silver ones with blue stars. Harley and Louie also covered the tree with crinkly silver icicles. Louie felt proud that he could help.

When they finished decorating the tree, they all stood back and watched while Harley plugged in the lights.

Marve said, "Now, that's some tree. I think it's beautiful." They all agreed.

Finally, the day before Christmas arrived. The Hooker home overflowed with delicious aromas. Mum baked spicy, apple pies that smelled of cinnamon. She rolled out thin, flaky pie crusts with her rolling pin that had a handle on only one end. Mum liked that rolling pin best.

Mum made extra pie crust on purpose. She knew that Louie and his brothers and sisters liked to eat the extra crust with sugar on it. Virginia cut the crust that was left over from the pies into thin strips. Then she placed them into the oven of the kitchen stove. After baking, she took the strips out of the oven, placed them on the counter and sprinkled sugar on them. Louie placed his nose above the flaky strips and sniffed.

Virginia warned, "Get back, Louie, or you'll burn your nose."

The pie crust strips smelled so good. It was so hard to wait. Soon they cooled, and each of them ate a small, tasty strip.

Louie said, "I want more!"

Virginia remarked, "We'll have to share and cut the last three strips into pieces."

They were so crisp that she had to break them with her fingers. Then they each had a small piece. The sugary crust seemed to melt in Louie's mouth.

Mum was busy kneading some bread dough while this was going on. She had a big ball of dough. It took a lot of bread to feed a family of eight. Mum made delicious bread and rolls. She punched and rolled the dough. Louie smelled the yeast that Mum added to make the bread rise. After kneading the dough for some time, Mum cut the dough into small chunks the size of a bar of soap. Then she placed the chunks into a large pan, side by side, for buns. She also cut some larger chunks and put them into loaf pans for loaves.

After letting the buns and loaves rise and become larger, she placed them in the oven for baking. Oh how good they smelled! Mum let Louie and his brothers each sample one-half a bun when they came out of the oven. Louie watched the butter melt on the hot bun. Then he bit a small piece. The piece of bun with melted butter rolled around his tongue before he swallowed it. He wished it lasted forever.

On this day before Christmas, Virginia popped some popcorn. She poured some caramel over the popcorn. Before shaping the caramel popcorn into balls, she put some shortening on her hands so it wouldn't stick to her hands.

"May we eat a popcorn ball?" asked Louie.

"No," answered Virginia, "They are for the Christmas stockings."

Louie, Harley and younger brother, Les, were disappointed, but Virginia let them slicker out the caramel pan.

All the Hooker kids were acting secretive that afternoon and into the evening. They hurriedly wrapped presents and placed them under the tree when no one was looking.

Shortly before bed time, the whole family entered the "front room" and gathered around the Christmas tree. The lights on the tree were sparkling - green, red, blue and gold. The pine branches gave off a smell of pine. Louie's heart was bursting with all the excitement and anticipation. He sat on one of Dad's knees, Les on the other. Louie stared at the many gifts under the tree - he wanted to know which presents were his and what they were.

Then Dad got everyone's attention. He began reciting "Twas the Night Before Christmas". He didn't need a book, he knew it from memory. "...........On Comet, On Cupid, On Donner and Blitzen." Louie could picture the reindeer prancing on the rooftop of the big, white Hooker home.

Then the entire family sang "Silent Night". Louie didn't know some of the words, but he hummed along if he didn't know them. Les just sat and listened.

Soon it was bed time for all the kids. On that Christmas Eve in 1941, Louie had a difficult time going to sleep. All the presents, good smelling foods and stockings filled with candy and nuts were so exciting.

One custom that the Hooker family had each Christmas morning was to see who could beat the other saying "Merry Christmas."

Marve thought of a clever way to beat Virginia. He set his alarm clock for shortly after midnight. He placed his pillow over the clock to muffle the sound so no one else would awaken.

Just after midnight, Louie heard a faint tinkling sound. He wondered what it was. He heard Marve stealthily creeping out of his bedroom toward Virginia's room. Marve was intending to beat Virginia at the "Merry Christmas" game while she was still sleeping.

Suddenly, Louie heard Virginia say, "Merry Christmas, Marve".

"Oh, you beat me again!" screamed Marve.

Soon there was a lot of laughing and noisy talking. All the kids upstairs were awake. There were many "Merry Christmas" greetings.

Finally, Dad yelled from the bottom of the stairs, "You kids better get to sleep. Morning will soon be here."

Chapter

6

Bowling Pins and Spools

One morning in the winter after he got burned, Louie sat up in bed to the sound of a high, shrill noise. It sounded like a church organ. The sound went up and down in pitch.

Was it music on the radio downstairs? Then he realized it was the wind outside. The bedroom upstairs which Louie shared with his brother, was very cold. In fact, sometimes it was so cold upstairs there was ice in the pot which was used for the winter bathroom.

Louie shivered as he threw the heavy blankets aside. His feet hit the cold linoleum floor. He looked for his brother, but Harley had gone to school. Marve and Harley had walked to school before the storm began. They attended Brookside School. It was down the road over two miles away.

When Louie got to the bottom of the stairway, Mum was standing by the register that brought heat from the big wood furnace in the basement. Mum often stood there on cold winter mornings to warm herself.

"Good morning, Louie," she said. He could hardly hear her, even though he stood very near. The wind outside made so much noise. "How do you like the sound of that wind?"

"I'm cold," Louie responded. Then he snuggled into Mum's skirt. The heat from the furnace sure felt good on his bare ankles.

Mum said, "You better put on your long underwear, shirt and bib overalls so you don't get cold."

Louie didn't like long, wool underwear, because it pricked and made his skin itch. But he knew he must wear it to keep warm.

He quickly dressed and looked out the big, bay window on the north side of the dining room. He looked toward the barn, but he could not see it. The wind was blowing the snow in big, white sheets straight across the ground. He couldn't even see the windmill less than fifty feet away. At that moment, the wind howled fiercely, sounding like a pack of wolves.

Louie said, "I want to go out to the barn after I eat breakfast to watch Dad clean out the gutters." A gutter is a ditch made of cement located behind the cattle where they stood in their stalls. It caught the manure. The cows stood side by side with only a small bar to separate them.

"Why no, you would get lost in the wind and snow before you get there. You sit down now and eat your breakfast and then I will set up a pretend barn for you."

"Okay."

Mum fed him some puffed wheat cereal with sugar and milk for breakfast. After that she went to a kitchen drawer and took out some cardboard. She cut the cardboard into small pieces about three inches square.

"What are you going to do with those?" asked Louie.

"Wait and see," answered Mum.

From the toy box in the dining room, she got some Ten Pins and spools. Ten Pins were small pins from a bowling game. The empty spools were from thread that Mum had used in the sewing machine. Then she took some wooden blocks from the toy box and set them in a row on the dining room floor. She placed the little pieces of cardboard between the blocks. This made little stalls for animals, like in the barn. She placed some Ten Pins in some of the spaces and the spools in others.

"Now," she said to Louie, "The Ten Pins are cows and the spools are horses."

"Oh, this looks like fun," said Louie.

He picked up a pin and marched it with a tap-tap-tap across the linoleum floor. Then he took a pretend horse and tapped that across the floor to a make believe pasture. The pasture was soon full of pins and spools, cows and horses.

"Look, Mum, all the cows and horses are in the pasture."

Mum said, "Now, isn't that almost as much fun as going out to the barn to watch Dad?"

"Yes, I like it."

Just then the telephone rang in the kitchen. It was Mr. Melton, the principal at Brookside School. He said they were dismissing school at noon because of the storm.

Dad had just finished the chores in the barn. When he came through the door, Mum met him to tell him that he had to pick up the kids from school.

"Well," Dad said, "I better hitch up the horses."

Louie wanted to go along with Dad so bad. "Please, may I go along, Dad?" he asked.

"No," answered Dad, "You better stay home. Your legs are still weak, and I wouldn't want to risk getting stuck in a snow bank. Then you'd have to walk. You know how your burns itch if they get cold."

There were tears in Louie's eyes as Dad shut the door to go to the barn.

When Dad stepped into the barn, Dick and Don, the two brown horses perked up their ears. They were always eager to get outside and stretch their legs during the winter.

"Would you like to go out and pull the sleigh?" Dad asked the horses.

Don gave a whinny as if he understood. Dad hitched them to the sleigh. They were soon on their way toward Brookside School. Dad had put on his horsehair coat to protect himself from the wind. He also brought along lots of blankets to wrap around the kids to protect them from the wind.

When Dad arrived at the school, all the kids were huddled anxiously at the door.

As Dad came to the door, Marve said, "Are we ever glad to see you, Dad. We thought we might have to sleep in the school tonight."

The kids hurriedly put on their coats and boots and ran out to the sleigh. Graydon and Ben Frens jumped on the sleigh too. They were neighbors that lived on the same road as the Hooker family.

When they arrived home, the kids burst noisily into the house. Harley said, "We saw a Model A Ford stuck in a snow bank on the corner by our church. Dad and Marve helped push him out of the snow bank."

Dad and the others had something to add about their cold trip home through the snow and cold wind. They could hear it screeching outside as they talked.

Mum fixed them some hot chocolate and gave them some of her homemade peanut butter cookies. It seemed so snug and comfortable as they sat around the kitchen table near the stove. The Hooker family was all safe in their big, white farm house.

Louie had a hard time waiting for them to finish their hot chocolate and cookies. He finally said to Harley, "Come with me and look at the play barn that Mum made for me." They hurried into the dining room.

Louie showed him the pretend barn. "These are horses and cows."

"They are not," said Harley, "They're only Ten Pins and spools."

Louie argued, "Mum said the Ten Pins stood for cows and the spools stood for horses."

Harley agreed if Mum said so. Then they played with their pretend farm for quite some time.

Les joined them and played with the pretend farm too. Virginia and Marve worked on a jigsaw puzzle. They spent the whole afternoon playing while the wind howled outside.

That night the wind was still screeching when Louie went to bed and snuggled under his heavy blankets. He felt safe and snug. He wrapped his pillow around his head so he couldn't hear the howling wind.

The next morning the wind had quieted, and Louie went outside to play in the big snow drifts. He remembered how Mum had taught him to play with Ten Pins and spools, but playing outside was still more fun.

Chapter

7

Sundays

Winter days seemed to pass so slowly for Louie at the Hooker farm. He liked to play outside, but cold and snow made it so he had to stay inside. Sundays were different. On Sundays the whole family was all together, and this made the day more interesting and exciting. Usually Louie went to church twice on Sundays, morning and afternoon. On some Sundays, he did not go in the morning, because the service was spoken and sung in Dutch. Many people of the church at Reeman could speak and read Dutch. They had one morning service a month in Dutch.

Saturday night was bath night. Dad put a big, laundry tub in the center of the "little kitchen". The "little kitchen" was located just off from the main kitchen. It had a sink and a washing machine. Dad put warm water in the laundry tub from a tank that was attached to the kitchen stove. The tank was called the reservoir. The water from this tank was used for Saturday night baths and washing clothes on Monday.

On Sunday morning, everyone in the Hooker family awakened early. After Dad, Marve and Harley finished chores, everyone sat down for a breakfast of cereal and milk with some bacon. The family had to hurry to make the 9:30 service at the Reeman Church.

After breakfast, Mum said, "Harley and Louie, put on a clean shirt and your knickers." Knickers were pants that reached down only to your knees. Long stockings were worn to cover the legs from the knees to the ankles. Louie thought they looked kind of silly. The boys also had to wear a flat hat with a short, little brim.

"Hurry up now, everyone!" said Dad as he hurried out the door to start the 1937 Ford. When Mum and the kids did not come soon enough, Dad would honk on the horn to remind everyone to hurry.

All nine of the Hooker family piled into the car. Louie, Les and Corrine sat between the legs of the older kids in the back seat. Mum held Dale, who was only one month old, in the front seat. Dale was born in January of 1942. Then Dad drove the car quite fast to the church, a half mile up the road.

The second bell was already ringing; the Hookers were late again. The custodian rang the bell at 9:00, and a second time at 9:25 on Sunday mornings.

Dad was in the consistory. The consistory was a group of men that helped Rev. Goodling guide the Reeman Church.

As they piled out of the car, Dad hastily said, "Louie, you come with me and sit with the consistory." The men on the consistory filed in church separately and sat on two benches facing the side of the pulpit in front of church. Louie felt important that he had been chosen to sit with the consistory. He really had to sit with Dad, because Mum couldn't handle all the Hooker kids alone during the service.

Louie sometimes had a hard time sitting still.

That day Rev. Goodling preached a long sermon. Louie got restless. He counted all the ceiling tiles. He stopped counting when he got to eighty-nine, because he couldn't count any farther. Then he chewed into tiny pieces a pink peppermint. Each of the children of the Hooker family took four peppermints to church for a treat. Crunch – Crunch – Crunch – Crunch!

Dad looked sternly at Louie and whispered quite loudly, "Louie, don't make so much noise chewing your candy."

Then Louie fiddled around with the nickel that was in his pocket for the collection. He took it out and looked at the buffalo on the one side. He wondered if there was another animal on the other side. Oops! He dropped it on the hard wooden floor. It rolled all the way to the communion table in front of the pulpit. Everyone was looking at Louie. His face turned many colors of red; he felt so foolish.

Louie noticed Harley was pointing at the nickel on the floor. Then Harley made funny faces at him. Of course, this made him even more embarrassed and mad.

When the service was over, Louie was glad he could go home and not have people ask him about the nickel.

The Sunday noon meal was pea soup with crackers. It usually was something that Mum could prepare quickly.

After the meal was finished and dishes done, Mum and Dad took a nap. The kids played games.

Soon Dad yelled from the bedroom, "Hey, kids, stop playing with the marble roller, it's too noisy!" The marble roller was made of wood and had little troughs, or alleys, that slanted downward from the top to the bottom. Marbles could be put in the top alley, and they would drop into each alley downward until they reached the bottom. Clatter – Clatter – Clatter! What a noise! The house seemed so quiet when they stopped the game. Mum and Dad finished their nap.

The Hooker family went to church again in the afternoon. Often Virginia stayed home with Corrine and Dale.

After evening chores, Dad said, "Let's play Ten Pins. Marve, would you go to the toy box and find the game?"

When Marve returned with the game, everyone went into the kitchen. The table was pushed aside to make room to set up the pins and roll the balls. Ten Pins was a game like bowling which was played on a hard linoleum floor. The entire family took turns competing against each other. Afterwards a champion was declared. Harley won the most games that night.

After the games, Louie said excitedly, "Dad, let's pop some popcorn."

"That's a good idea," responded Dad. "Harley and Marve, will you go to the shed and get some popcorn?" Dad grew popcorn every summer, and the ears of popcorn were stored in the shed. They were in a crate on the top of a metal barrel. The barrel protected the popcorn from the mice, because they couldn't climb up its steep sides.

The boys soon returned with fifteen ears of popcorn. Dad shelled the popcorn from the ears. His hands were hard and calloused. He could shell the corn easily without hurting his hands. Louie tried too, but soon his hands had speckles of blood where the sharp kernels pierced his skin.

Dad placed a large frying pan on the hot kitchen stove. He poured some bacon grease and one-half cup of the shelled popcorn into the pan. Dad held a cover over the frying pan and slid the hot pan back and forth across the top of the stove. Beads of sweat appeared on his forehead. Making popcorn was hot work.

Pop - pop - pop, the kernels were popping. Soon the pan was so full the cover almost burst off the top. Oh! It smelled good as he poured the steamy white kernels into a large, clean dishpan. Shortly, the dishpan was full and Dad announced, "The popcorn is ready, come and get it."

The entire family sat around the kitchen table. They all scooped some popcorn from the dishpan and made a pile in front of themselves. Then each ate from their pile until a refill was needed from the dishpan. Each

person had a glass of water to slosh it down.

Harley said, "Louie, you took some popcorn from my pile. Mum, make Louie eat his own popcorn."

Mum looked sternly at Louie and said, "Louie, you must not tease. Now eat from your own pile, there's plenty for everyone."

After everyone had eaten their fill, it was bedtime. Another interesting Sunday had come and gone at the big, white Hooker farm house.

Chapter

8

Butchering

One morning, in the winter after Louie got burned, he rose early because he knew Dad was going to butcher a big hog that day. This was his first time to watch butchering, and he didn't want to miss it for anything. After a quick breakfast, he went outside by the little chicken coop. Uncle Edd, Louie's Great Uncle, was already there to help Dad butcher. He lived up the road near Brookside School.

"Boy, you're up early," said Uncle Edd to Louie.

"Yah," said Louie, "I want to watch the butchering. It's my first time."

"How are your legs doing?" asked Uncle Edd. Uncle Edd had visited Louie often during his time of recovery.

"Oh, okay. They kinda itch though, from the cold."

Before Uncle Edd arrived, Dad told Louie that he had dumped many pails of water into a huge iron pot that was located on one end of the big chicken coop. He said he had built a wood fire under and around the pot to heat the water. The pot of water was already bubbling.

"Well," said Dad to Uncle Edd, "I guess we're ready to kill the hog."

Louie shivered at the thought of killing a pig, but he was determined to watch. He followed closely behind the men as they approached the pigpen.

Dad used an old rifle and took careful aim. He shot the hog between the eyes. The pig squealed.

Louie's face showed alarm. He began to run toward the house. He stopped. He wanted to be brave, so he ambled slowly back toward the pigpen. The squealing gradually stopped.

Then Uncle Edd and Dad put the hog on a long wooden frame that had two handles on each end. Uncle Edd grabbed the two handles on one end. Dad grabbed the two on the other end. They lifted the heavy hog into the air and carried it to a place near the little chicken coop. There was a wooden platform there. Near the wooden platform was a large barrel with boiling water in it. Beforehand, Dad had dipped pails of boiling water from the big iron pot and poured them into the barrel.

The two men placed the hog on the platform. Then Dad put a wooden pole that was pointed on each end between the two back legs of the hog. He tied the pole to each leg of the pig with heavy cord.

Uncle Edd and Dad stood on the platform. They each grabbed hold of one end of the pointed pole between the hog's legs.

"Ready, Reen," asked Uncle Ed? This is what Uncle Ed called Dad; it was short for Myreenus.

"Yah," Dad answered.

Splish and splash, splish and splash, they dipped the hog head first into the boiling water. The hog was heavy, and it made the men grunt as they swished it up and down into the barrel of hot water. After some time, Uncle Edd placed the pointed pole between the front legs of the hog. Now they dipped the hog into the barrel hind feet first. Louie was too close, and he felt a drop of the hot water hit his face.

After quite some time of dipping the pig, they lay it flat on the platform. Dad said, "Let's check to see if the hog is ready for scraping." The hot water made the hair tender so it could be scraped easily. They tested the hog.

"I think she's ready," said Uncle Edd. Then the two men took little round scrapers with wooden handles to scrape the hair off the hog. They scraped and scraped. Bunches of hair fell on the ground around the platform. Louie felt the hair. It felt tough and bristly. It smelled like pig. He also touched the skin of the dead pig where the hair had been removed. It felt rubbery and cold. Louie shivered.

Uncle Edd and Dad put the scraped hog on a cart and wheeled it to the tool shed. Louie noticed that blood was still dripping from the hog's mouth as they pulled the cart. He tried to step around the spots of blood in the snow as he followed closely behind. At the tool shed the hog was fastened with some rope by its back legs to some wooden beams on the ceiling. This made the hog's head hang near the dirt floor. Louie stood very close watching every move of the two men.

"Don't get too close!" warned Dad, "We've got work to do." Then Uncle Edd and Dad used sharp butcher knives to cut out the insides of the hog. Louie didn't like the smell of the hog as they did this. He gagged. He held his nose with his fingers so he wouldn't get sick.

When they finished, Dad said, "There, we're done. Now we must let it hang for a couple of days to let it cool."

That night the Hooker family ate fried pig's heart and some hock (pig's feet) for supper. The hock contained a lot of fat with a large bone in the center. It was rather greasy tasting. Louie enjoyed eating all the different kinds of meat at butchering time. He also knew that Grandpa Tanis would be over in two days to help cut up the hog.

Chapter

9

Grandpa Tanis

Two days later, early in the morning, Louie looked out of the frosty window of his upstairs bedroom. Smoke was rising from the chimney on the milk house.

"Oh," thought Louie, "Today Grandpa Tanis is coming over to cut up the hog." Grandpa Tanis was Mum's stepfather. He had married Mum's mother after her first husband died. Louie, along with Harley and Les, hurried downstairs. Dad was already sitting at the kitchen table.

"Hurry and sit down, boys," he said, "Grandpa will be here soon, and we shouldn't make him wait." Dad said a prayer. Then the three boys gulped down a breakfast of eggs and toast that Mum had prepared.

It was hard for Louie to listen while Dad read from the "Daily Manna" devotional after the meal. He knew that Grandpa would soon arrive in his blue 1937 Dodge.

"Put on your Mackinaw coats, boys," said Mum. "It's cold out this morning." Mackinaws were heavy woolen coats that many people wore in those days.

Just as the boys stepped out the back door and were trudging through the new fallen snow toward the milk house, Grandpa drove in the driveway. The boys met him as he opened his car door.

"Hi," said Grandpa. "How come you boys are up so early?"

"Oh, we want to watch you cut up the pig," answered Louie. They walked quickly toward the milk house. The winter wind made them shiver.

The back part of the milk house had a small room with a sturdy wooden table on one side. On the other side was a large stove called a range. The range could be used for cooking and baking. It also kept the milk house warm.

Dad came through the back door of the milk house carrying a big piece of meat. It was the back part of a hog. Dad called it "The Hind Quarter."

Lay it here on the table, Reen" said Grandpa. Grandpa began cutting the meat. Harley, Louie and Les watched his every move. Grandpa was very careful and fussy with his work. He kept his long butcher knife very sharp. Sometimes he used a big meat saw to cut through a bone.

After some time, Les said, "I'm going to the house to play with some Tinker Toys."

Dad peeked through the door and said, "Harley, it's time to do the barn chores." Louie was glad he was too young to help with chores. Now, he was alone with Grandpa.

Sometime later that morning, Grandpa cut off the tail of the hog. He wrapped it in paper and tied a string around it.

"Here, Louie," he said with a twinkle in his eye. "Take this to your Mum for a present." Louie had been waiting for this. Grandpa had done the same thing last year. It was so much fun.

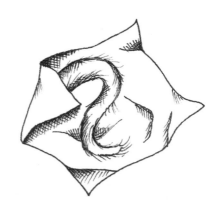

He ran through the snow to the house. Mum met him at the door.

"What is my little boy hiding behind his back?" she asked. Mum acted surprised, even though Louie had brought the same present to her the year before.

"It's really a nice present," said Louie as he could hardly hold back a giggle.

Mum unwrapped it slowly. Louie had a hard time waiting.

"Oh my! It's a pig's tail!" she gasped.

Louie laughed loudly. He thought Mum was so easy to fool.

Chapter

10

Peppy the Pony

The big snows of winter were over. The bright sun beamed on the Hooker farm. It was so wonderful to feel the warm sun and see patches of brown earth and grass. The sap began to flow up the trunks of the maple trees in the pasture. Dad got out all of the equipment he used for collecting maple sap.

One day Dad said, "Boys, tomorrow we'll go into the pasture and tap the maple trees. I'm expecting some clear, cool nights and more bright sunshine in the next few days." Maple sap begins to move to the upper branches of the tree when the late winter nights are cool and the days sunny. The sap helps the trees to bud and make leaves in the spring.

Harley and Louie's ears perked up when they heard Dad's announcement of maple sap. They enjoyed getting outside after the winter days that seemed so long. It was fun to watch Dad tap the maple trees.

Harley whistled to Peppy, the family's small black and white fox terrier. "Hey, Peppy, are you ready for me to hitch you to your cart?"

Peppy seemed to sense exactly what Harley was talking about. His ears stood up straight; he wagged his tail and gave Harley's hand a nuzzle. Peppy was a spirited dog, even when he was a puppy. Harley had built a little cart for Peppy to pull. He also had made a tiny harness from leather that fit Peppy's small body. Harley had trained Peppy to pull the cart just like a farmer trained his horses to pull a wagon. So, when Harley talked to Peppy about his cart, he gave a little "Yip" to say yes.

The next day Dad took his wood drill and the spigots to place in each tree in the pasture. Harley and Louie, along with Peppy, followed closely at Dad's heels. When they got to a big maple tree, Dad drilled a hole into the trunk of the tree and pushed a spigot into the hole. A spigot was a little piece of wood shaped like a trough, or a tiny, curved ditch, through which the sap could flow. The sap would flow from the trunk of the tree through the wooden spigot into a bucket that hung on the tree.

Louie said to Dad, "Doesn't that hurt the tree when you drill into it?"

"No," answered Dad, "After the sap season is over, the tree quickly heals itself and prepares for next year's sap season."

That night was clear, cold and crisp. Frost was hanging on the trees in the morning. The sun shined brilliantly over the pasture to the east of the farm buildings.

Harley and Louie rose early. After breakfast, they were eager to check the maple sap buckets. Peppy knew that today was a different day too. He stayed near the boys during breakfast. They would slip him a small crumb of liver worst whenever Mum wasn't looking. Then Peppy gave a little "Yip" for more, and Mum heard him.

"Now, boys, I've told you before, you shouldn't feed Peppy at the table." Louie gave Mum a sheepish grin as he and Harley finished their breakfast.

After breakfast, the boys went outside and soon had Peppy hitched to his cart. The cart held two pails in which to dump the buckets of sap. Peppy looked pert and proud. Harley held the leash that was attached to Peppy's collar. They headed toward the pasture with Louie following behind the cart.

Just past the big chicken coop, Peppy began to flounder in a big snow bank. The cart got stuck in the bank. It was too hard to pull. Peppy began to balk; he twisted and turned in his harness. The harness got all tangled around his head, and he gave his normal Peppy growl when Harley tried to straighten it. The two boys soon had Peppy untangled and walked at a fast pace toward the trees in the pasture.

The first bucket was nearly full. Louie said to Harley, "May I dump the first bucket?" Harley agreed, and Louie carefully took the bucket from the nail on the tree and dumped it into a pail on the cart behind Peppy. He stood obediently, waiting for Louie to finish. Then Harley led him from tree to tree until the boys had emptied all the buckets. The two large pails on the cart were nearly full. Harley led Peppy

slowly through the banks of snow and over the bumps in the pasture so the sap would not spill.

Louie walked behind and sometimes steadied the cart when it tipped.

When the boys and Peppy arrived home, Mum poured the sap in a large blue kettle with white spots and placed it on the kitchen stove. All day long the sap boiled, and steam went into the air. By night, there was only a small amount of sap left in the kettle. It was quite thick and brown.

Mum said, "The Maple syrup is almost ready. We can have maple syrup on pancakes for supper." All the kids in the kitchen let out a big "Hurrah!" There was nothing better than fluffy, brown pancakes with fresh, hot maple syrup.

Peppy was tired and went behind the kitchen stove to get warm and sleep.

The Hooker family enjoyed a wonderful supper of pancakes with maple syrup that night. Mum also fixed some metworst sausage to eat with the pancakes. Metworst was a special sausage that Mum and Dad made at butchering time. Louie even had a second and third helping of metworst and pancakes.

Each day after that for several weeks, Harley, Louie and Peppy went faithfully out to the pasture to collect maple sap. Mum boiled the sap for many days. The family had a good supply of maple syrup to last through the summer and winter until the next maple sap season.

Chapter

11

Baby Chicks

Spring days and nights were exciting times around the Hooker farm. Many baby animals arrived. Baby calves and litters of pigs were born.

One day in March, Mum yelled up the stairway to Louie and Les, "Boys, you should get up! If you want to see the baby chicks arrive, you better be ready!"

Louie and Les hurried downstairs.

After eating a quick breakfast, they headed out the back door of the big, white house. The sun was shining brightly. The snow was all melted, except for a few spots where there had been some big drifts.

The boys ran to the brooder coop. The brooder coop was where Dad placed the little chicks when they arrived.

Dad met them at the door and said, "Boys, you're just in time to help me get everything ready for our babies to arrive."

Dad had prepared two rooms with a brooder in each. Brooders looked like large, metal umbrellas close to the floor. There were electric heat coils in the brooders to keep the chicks warm. They also had light bulbs for heat and light. Three hundred chicks could be placed under one brooder and two hundred under the other. The brooders acted like giant mother hens waiting to receive their babies.

As the boys stepped into the coop, Louie said, "Dad, I want to help put feed in the feeders."

"Okay, Louie, you carry the pails. Les, you put two small scoops in each feeder."

There was starter mash, which is ground up grain, in one pail and oatmeal in the other. Louie watched Les carefully to make sure he didn't spill any of the feed.

Dad was filling little waterers for the chicks to drink from while the boys were doing this.

"There," said Dad, "We're ready for our babies."

Just then they could hear the crunching of tires on the driveway outside the brooder coop.

The boys scurried to the doorway and saw Mr. Delbart's green truck rolling to a stop.

Mr. Delbart opened the truck door and said, "Hello boys, I brought you five hundred babies."

"Yippee!" responded Louie, "We're all ready for them."

Mr. Delbart opened the back doors of his truck. The boys saw many boxes with round holes in them. Through the holes they could see tiny, beady, black eyes and little yellow beaks. The holes in the boxes provided air for the baby chicks to breathe.

The boys stepped up close and stuck their fingers through the little holes. One little chick pecked Les' finger.

There were ten boxes of chicks with fifty chicks in each box.

Dad said, "These chicks are baby Leghorns. Leghorns lay lots of eggs when they get older."

Mr. Delbart and Dad carried the boxes of chicks near the brooders. They carefully lifted chicks out of the boxes and placed them by the edge of the brooders. They scuttled under the brooders. Some of them began pecking at the oatmeal and mash.

Dad said to Louie and Les, "You may each take ten chicks carefully from the box."

Then Louie yelled to Les, "Be careful! Pick them up under their bodies!" The sound of Louie's loud voice made the chicks huddle in little bunches in fear.

Dad warned the boys, "Don't yell or make loud noises. It scares the chicks and makes them bunch together. They may smother each other. Speak softly."

Soon they had placed all the fluffy, little chicks under their brooders. They were happily eating from their small feeders and drinking from their tiny waterers. An occasional loud peep was heard when one stepped on another.

After Mr. Delbart left, Dad, Louie and Les walked to the house for morning lunch. Dad informed them, "In five months those little chicks will start laying eggs."

Throughout the next few weeks, Louie often went to the brooder coop. He picked up little chicks and let them eat from his hand. He wished they would stay tiny forever.

Chapter

12

Rats in the Stack

"It's time to finish up the corn stack and get the rats this morning," said Dad one Saturday morning at the breakfast table.

It was early spring. In the fall, Dad had neatly put the husked corn stalks in a big stack between the barn and driveway. Throughout the winter, the bundles of cornstalks were brought into the barn and fed to the cattle. The cows munched on the brown leaves of corn so that none of it was wasted. The stack was nearly gone. Only three rows of bundles were left on the bottom.

Many rats made the stack their home during the winter. There was plenty of food for them in the corn stack, and it made a cozy home for them. Some of the stalks even had small ears of corn that had not been husked. The rats were sneaky throughout the winter, and Louie never saw any. But, he often saw their tracks in the new fallen snow near the stack.

"Come on, Peppy," shouted Louie to their little fox terrier, "Let's get the rats!"

Peppy was eager for excitement. He didn't like rats; he loved to kill them. So, when Louie called, he was excited and ready.

The Hooker family had another dog named Buster. He was larger than Peppy and was black and brown. Peppy was the leader, and Buster usually followed. When Louie called to Peppy, Buster came following behind him.

Dad and all the boys of the family, except Dale, went out the door and hurried to the stack of corn. The dogs were barking. They were bristling with excitement.

Dad shouted, "Marve, open the big sliding doors to the barn floor. We'll put the last three rows of bundles from the stack on the barn floor."

Everyone knew that many rats were hiding under the last few bundles. Peppy could smell them, and he began to run in circles around the stack. He would stop and sniff as he circled it. His hair was standing up on the scruff of his neck. He barked excitedly. He could hardly wait for Marve, Dad and Harley to lift the bundles.

"Listen," shouted Dad, "Louie, you hold Peppy on the side of the stack toward the barn. Les, you hold Buster on the side toward the shed. That way we have the two most important sides of the stack covered."

Rats usually run toward a building, or cover of some kind, when they are exposed. Dad wanted the dogs to catch and kill them before they escaped to the barn or shed.

Louie grabbed Peppy by the collar to hold him on the barn side. Peppy was nervous. He pulled at the collar and wanted to be free. Louie held him firmly by his side.

Les stood on the other side toward the shed, poised and ready, with Buster.

"Okay, here we go!" shouted Dad as he lifted a bundle of corn and headed toward the barn. Marve picked up another bundle. Harley grabbed a third bundle. Harley dragged his bundle toward the barn. It was too heavy for him to lift and carry all the way to the barn.

No rats ran from the stack when they lifted the first bundles of corn. They were still hiding under the bottom row of cornstalks.

Peppy tugged harder at his collar. He wanted loose. He could smell rats. Louie dug his heels in the dirt and held tightly so Peppy would be at the right spot.

Les was having an easier time with Buster. Even though Buster was bigger than Peppy, he was easier to handle.

"I think I saw a rat's tail under that next bundle," hollered Dad, "Be ready!"

Dad grabbed the string that held the bundle together and lifted it from the stack. A big gray rat scuttled from under the bundle. It headed straight toward Louie and Peppy.

"Let Peppy go!" yelled Dad.

Louie released Peppy. He chased the big rat as it headed toward a hole on the side of the barn. Peppy was faster. Just before it reached the barn, he sunk his teeth into the rat. His little jaw was strong, and he held the rat firmly in his mouth.

"Squeak, Squeak!" screamed the rat.

"Yip, Yip!" yapped Peppy.

Peppy had the rat by its hind legs in his mouth. He shook his head violently back and forth, back and forth. The rat was trying to bite him. He shook the rat harder and harder.

The rat was squeaking less and less. With a final big shake, Peppy laid the large rat on a mound of dirt. The rat was still quivering, but it was dying.

Louie walked up to Peppy. His tail was wagging, and he looked first at Louie and then at his prized rat. Peppy had won the battle.

Louie patted his head and said, "Good dog, you sure took care of that old rat!"

"Oh, Peppy!" screamed Louie, "You're bleeding on your nose. Let me look at it!"

Peppy didn't want to stand still for Louie to look. He was too wound up, but Louie held tightly onto his collar.

After he checked Peppy's nose, he yelled, "There's a tooth from the rat stuck right in Peppy's nose!"

Harley investigated too and said, "Yes, there's a dirty brown tooth stuck right in Peppy's nose alright. The rat bit Peppy before he killed him. The rat's tooth broke off. But, Peppy was the winner."

Harley tried to pick the rat's tooth from Peppy's nose, but it slipped through his fingers. Dad said, "He will be alright, the tooth will work itself out of his nose.

Everyone gathered around Peppy and praised him for a job well done. He held his head high and wagged his tail - but, not for long. He had more rats on his mind.

Marve picked up another corn bundle, and three more rats ran in three different directions. Buster grabbed one, Peppy snatched another and the third rat escaped between the corncrib and the shed.

As they lifted each bundle, more rats emerged. The dogs killed many of them and only a few escaped.

When Marve lifted the last bundle, there were two final rats that the dogs were able to chase down and capture.

Dad said, "I think the dogs killed twelve rats and only four got away. I'm proud of our dogs and am happy they were able to kill most of the critters. The rats eat a lot of corn and grain that is stored for the cattle and hogs. They also do a lot of damage by chewing and ruining valuable items. Now our farm has become a better place."

Chapter

13

Boat Race

One night in June when Louie went to bed, it was raining very hard. The patter of the rain drops on the roof made a loud noise. It was difficult for him to get to sleep. It rained several inches throughout the night.

The next morning the wide drainage ditch just behind the pigpen was rushing with brown, swirling water. Marve, Harley and Louie went out to inspect the gushing stream.

Marve said, "Let's have a boat race." Harley and Louie thought that sounded exciting. It was something they did every year when the water was high. It was fun and thrilling.

They decided that each of them would pick a small piece of wood for their own personal boat for the race. Marve and Harley each chose a large, wooden stick about one foot long. Louie saw a tiny piece of wood that had been part of the pigpen fence. The fence had rotted, and a piece had fallen off. It was light brown in color and only about three inches long. Being rotted wood, it was very light.

"Okay," said Marve, "Give me your boats, and I will start them all together just below the bridge." The bridge crossed the drainage ditch outside the barnyard gate. Dad used the bridge to pass over the ditch with his farm machinery.

Marve got on his knees, leaned way over the edge of the bridge and carefully dropped the play boats into the swirling water. All three boats skidded with a burst of speed across the top of the water. The gushing water from the culvert gave the boats a quick start for the beginning of the race. A culvert is a metal tube through which the water passes.

Shortly, Louie's small boat got stuck in some sticks and leaves on the edge of the ditch. Louie cried, "It's not fair, my boat is stuck, and I can't reach it."

Harley took a long pole and broke it loose, so it once again floated down the ditch trailing the other two boats. A rule of the race was that if your boat got stuck, you could use a pole to release it. The others would yell "unfair" if you gave it a little shove too. So you only got it unstuck and that's all.

The three boats headed toward where the ditch went under the fence. This was the finish line. The first boat to float under the fence was the winner.

Marve and Harley laughed at Louie's little boat. Marve said, "Your boat is too tiny, Louie. We'll get to the fence before yours is only halfway."

Louie acted as if he had not heard Marve. He hurried to help his boat. It was stuck. He couldn't jump back and forth across the ditch as his two brothers, because his legs were stiff from his burn scars. So he watched his boat closely from just one side. He made sure to use the pole immediately if his boat got stuck.

Each surge of water caught Louie's little boat and pushed it faster and faster toward the fence. It passed the other boats. His brothers' boats were too heavy and got stuck very often. Louie's boat skipped around the log jams and sometimes seemed to fly over top of them.

"Come on, little boat," Louie coaxed his tiny boat. It twisted and turned as it rushed across the top of the brown, dirty water toward the finish line. Louie had a difficult time keeping up with it as he ran beside the rushing water.

He looked back and saw that his brothers were quite a ways farther back.

Oh, his boat was stuck, and he gave it a poke one last time before it reached the fence.

Soon Louie let out a yell, "Hurrah, my boat is the winner!" He ducked under the fence so he could hurry to catch his boat. His coat caught on the barbed wire which left a tear just behind his shoulder. This happened to him a lot. His burn scars made him stiff, and he couldn't bend very well. But he was glad to be alive and happy that he was able to enjoy fun times like this with his brothers.

About a minute later, Harley and Marve's boats floated slowly under the fence. Louie wanted to brag, but he remembered that his brothers were older and bragging would only bring trouble.

Chapter

14

The Gopher

There was lots of work for the boys on the Hooker farm during the summer months. There were weeds to pull, cows to milk, chickens to feed and barn gutters to clean. However, there was often time to play and have fun.

One afternoon Dad told Harley and Louie they could go fishing to Spring Creek. It was a hazy day with only a few wispy clouds in the sky to the west.

Harley said to Louie, "Let's take a gunny sack with us. Maybe when we are finished fishing, we can use it." Gunny sacks were made from coarse brown threads called burlap and were used to hold grain.

"What are we going to do with the bag?" asked Louie. Harley didn't respond and Louie was quite sure they wouldn't catch a fish so big that they needed a gunny sack.

The boys got their fishing poles and two pails for the fish. Louie thought that one pail would be enough, but Harley insisted on two.

The boys walked across the field to the east to cousin Hank's house. Hank was Harley's age, and he had a gully right behind his house. The gully had been formed by many years of water surging down the creek that lay at its bottom. It had steep hills on each side of the creek.

Hank wanted to join them, so he got his pole. The three of them hurried to the gully.

During the summer, there was little or no water in the creek right behind the barn. Harley, Louie and Hank walked past two big beechnut trees. They passed "Big Bear" which was a nickname given to a huge elm tree located at the bottom of the gully. They hiked to the place where Spring Creek came from the north and joined the gully. They noticed some good holes, or deep spots, in the creek where there was bound to be fish.

Louie took a worm out of the tin can and put it on his hook. His fishing pole was short and had a bend at the end. It was made from a limb of a box elder tree. He dashed over close to a big fishing hole in the creek. Water was swirling in a little circle where it tumbled over a log that crossed the creek.

Louie thought if he dangled his line just over the log, he might get a fish to bite his hook. He set the bobber two feet from the hook. The bobber hit the water with a kerplunk as it settled beside the log.

Cousin Hank was walking across the creek on the log to get to the other side. He lost his balance and almost tumbled into the water.

Louie was watching Hank and not his bobber. When he looked back to where his bobber should be, it wasn't there. He had a bite! He yanked on the pole. His foot slipped in the mud on the bank. He sat down with his butt in the mud. There was a splash near the log as he pulled. Then he lifted a pink bellied fish from the creek.

"Wow!" shouted Louie, "Look at the size of that fish! I think it's a horned ace!" The Hooker boys knew that if the fish had little horns above its eyes, it was a horned ace.

Harley and Hank came by Louie as he twisted the hook from the fish's mouth. Harley put water in one of the pails, and Louie tossed the big fish into the pail with a splash.

"That will make a nice fish for the barn tank when we get home," said Louie.

The three boys continued on down the creek toward Eightieth Street. They caught sheep fish, shiners and several more horned aces. The boys knew where the good fishing holes were. They had nearly thirty fish in the pail by the time they stopped fishing. They kept fresh water in the pail so the fish would be alive when they got home.

Just on the south side of Eightieth Street, Harley took the gunny sack from the front of his bib overalls. He called out, "Remember those gopher holes we saw over that hill by the dump? I think we can catch one."

"How we gonna do that?" asked Louie.

"Just do as I say," answered Harley. "Hank, take the empty pail and fill it with water from the creek. Louie, fill the worm can with water too."

The boys carried the water and gunny sack up the hill by the dump. Many people dumped their garbage and tin cans in a deep ditch right next to the road on Eightieth Street.

The hillside near the dump was dotted with gopher holes. Harley pointed out a gopher hole that had some fresh, damp dirt near it. A gopher had just dug the hole deeper into the sod and sand.

"Now, listen to me, so we do this right," shouted Harley. "Hank and Louie, you pour the water into this hole. The gopher will come up for air. I'll hold the bag over the hole when he comes out and catch him."

"Okay," echoed the two boys together.

First Louie poured the can of water. Then Hank poured the whole pail of water right afterwards. The water gurgled as it sloshed down the hole.

Harley immediately placed the open gunny sack over the hole. The boys waited. Soon Harley felt a bump against his hand through the sack. A gopher scurried from the hole into the sack as it gasped for a breath of air. Harley quickly tied a string around the top of the sack.

The boys took turns feeling the bump which was the gopher inside the bag. They jerked their hand back each time the gopher moved inside its prison.

"Hey, Louie, do you see now why I brought the gunny sack?" asked Harley.

"Yah," answered Louie. He thought he had such a clever big brother.

The boys hurried toward home with their prize in the bag. Harley and Louie parted with Hank at his house. Then they proceeded across the field to the west and home.

Harley let Louie take turns carrying the brown bag. Every so often the gopher would lurch in the bag, but their prisoner could not escape.

When the two boys arrived home, Louie dumped the fish in the barn tank. Three of the fish were dead, so he fed them to the cats.

Harley took the bag with the gopher under the willow trees. A metal cage was there. This cage had held many kinds of animals over the years, but was empty now.

Louie opened the lid on the top. Harley untied the string on the bag. He thrust the bag through the opening. He shook the bag, and out popped a striped gopher. The gopher scampered to one corner of the cage and sat nervously looking at the boys with beady eyes.

Louie went to the barn for some straw. Harley pulled some grass. They put the straw and grass into the cage for the gopher. They also placed a little shallow dish of water in the cage for the little furry animal.

"Let's name him Gus," said Louie. Harley approved.

Then the boys sat and watched Gus until Mum called them for supper.

Two days later Louie noticed that Gus was making a nest in the corner of the cage. Harley said, "I think Gus knows this is his home, and he wants it to be cozy.

The following morning, Harley, Louie and Les sat by the cage for a little while to watch Gus. Suddenly Les said, "Did you hear that little squeak from the corner of the cage where Gus made a nest?"

The three boys moved close to the nest at the corner of the cage. Louie grabbed a small stick and poked the nest gently through a hole in the corner of the cage.

Harley noticed something different about Gus. He said, "Doesn't Gus look skinnier?"

"Yes, he does," the other boys answered together.

Then Louie said, "Look at Gus' tummy, it's wet in spots."

Harley grinned and said, "I think Gus had babies, and those wet spots are where the babies nursed."

The boys watched the gopher as she slowly walked back to her nest. They heard several more squeaks and knew that surely Gus had a family.

Suddenly Louie burst out, "Hey, we have to change Gus' name to a girl's name. She's a mother."

Harley thought for a short time. Then he said, "How about Gert? That starts with a G."

Les and Louie thought that was just fine.

So, from then on, it was not Gus the Gopher, but Gert the Gopher.

Chapter

15

Barnyard Game

One warm summer day that year, Louie's cousins, Richard and Doug, visited from Kalamazoo. They had not visited the Hooker farm since Louie had been burned. Their father was Uncle Joe. He was an older brother of Louie's dad. Their mother was Aunt Mildred. It was always a cheerful time when they came to visit. Uncle Joe was a school principal. He knew how to talk to kids. Aunt Mildred was so sweet and pleasant. Richard was Harley's age, and Doug was Les' age.

"Let's go to the barnyard to play," Harley called to Richard.

"Yah, that would be fun," he answered.

They climbed over the fence between the barn tank and the corn crib. Louie followed, but since his legs were still sore, it took him longer. But he did not want to miss out on any fun. Les and Doug went to play under the willow trees in the backyard.

There were about twenty black and white cows in the barnyard. The two brown horses, Dick and Don, were also there. They all stared at the boys with nervous eyes. They had never seen Richard before. Strange people make barnyard animals uneasy.

As they walked through the barnyard, Harley stepped over a fresh cow flop on the sand. One of the cows had pooped.

"I have an idea that might be some fun," he said to Richard and Louie.

"What is it?" asked Richard.

"Let's play a trick on Les with this big cow flop," he answered. "We'll cover the flop with nice brown sand so you can't even see it. Then we'll make a big pile of only sand right beside it."

"How will that trick Les?" asked Louie.

"You just wait and see," answered Harley with a grin on his face. Harley was mischievous and liked to trick others. He carefully covered the cow flop with brown sand so that it could not be seen. Harley told Louie to make a big pile of just sand nearby. The cows and horses were nosing nearer, getting braver each moment.

"Now for some fun," Harley said as he ran to the fence. Les and Doug were playing near the milk house.

Harley yelled, "Hey, Les, do you want to have some fun playing a new game with us?" Les liked games of all kinds, so he came eagerly. Doug was right at his heels. They climbed over the fence and came into the barnyard.

Harley said to Les, "Boy, is this fun to jump in piles of sand. Watch me do it." Harley ran fast and took a big leap and slid into the pile of sand. "Come on, Les, you can jump into the other pile," he called. "See if you can slide farther than I did."

Les felt proud that he had been chosen to jump into the other pile. He ran as fast as his little legs could move. He liked the challenge. When he reached the pile of sand, he slid with all his might. He hit more than sand. His bare feet hit oozy, green cow poop. His feet and back were completely covered. The other boys laughed so hard they tumbled on the ground.

Les felt his legs and pulled back his hand with a jerk. His hand was all dirty. He let out a scream and began crying.

"I'm going to tell Mum that you got poop all over me," cried Les. He ran toward the house with the other boys following.

As he came through the door, Mum said, "What happened to you?"

"Harley played a trick on me. He got cow poop all over me," cried Les.

Mum looked sternly at Harley and ordered, "You got him dirty, now you clean him up."

Harley picked up Les and carried him to the barn tank from which the cows drank. Les was kicking and fighting to get away. He threw him in with a splash. Les splashed around screaming and crying. Finally, he dragged himself from the tank. He was not much cleaner and still stunk. Again he ran crying to the house. Mum told him to leave his clothes at the door. Les didn't want to take his clothes off, not in front of visitors. But he didn't want to smell like cow poop either. So he took off his clothes, except for his underwear and dashed into the house. This time he took a bath in the big laundry tub.

The new game had not been what he had expected. Even though Harley had to do extra chores that night, Les thought he had gotten the dirtier end of the deal.

Chapter

16

Threshing Day

The summer of 1942 Dad made sure that every part of his eighty acre farm was used to produce crops. Dad said, "America is at war, and we must grow food for our country's soldiers."

Dad grew a large field of peas. Gerber Baby Foods in Fremont used them to make baby food.

He grew lots of potatoes on some sandy soil north of the barn. The Hooker family, now numbering nine, ate lots of potatoes. In April, Dad had taken the seed potatoes from the bin in the basement. Louie had helped Harley and Marve take the sprouts off the potatoes before Dad planted them.

The hay was already in the barn for winter. The corn was standing tall and green. The wheat was brown, ready for harvesting.

One week in July, Dad and Marve cut the wheat with the binder. It was pulled by the horses. The binder cut the wheat and bound it into a neat bundle with a strong twine holding it together. After cutting the wheat, Dad and Marve stacked the wheat in shocks. They made a shock of wheat by using ten bundles. The bundles were stacked closely together by twos leaning against each other. The bundles stood upright on the ground with their heads, or grain part, on top. The grain had to dry for a period of time, and Dad hoped that it would not rain.

About a week later in the morning when Louie sat up in bed, he could smell the wonderful aroma of freshly baked pies. He remembered, "Mum is preparing food for the men who will help Dad thresh wheat today."

The farmers in the neighborhood helped each other thresh. No farmer could ever do it alone.

Louie jumped out of bed and hustled downstairs. He saw rows of chicken drumsticks, breasts and wings lying on the kitchen counter. Mum and Virginia were preparing to bake them for the noon meal.

Harley was already at the breakfast table. The boys got their own breakfast on this busy morning. They ate hastily and ran out the door. They wanted to make sure they wouldn't miss the coming of the threshing machine.

The boys ran to sit under the apple trees near the edge of the garden. They pushed some yellow apples out of the way, so they wouldn't sit in partly rotten apples. Dad called the summer apples "Yellow Transparents".

As they sat down, Louie said to Harley, "Do you hear that Chug – Chug – Chug?"

"Yes," answered Harley, "That's Mr. Riggles' oil-burning tractor that pulls the threshing machine."

At that time, Les came out of the door of the house and joined Harley and Louie under the apple trees.

The three boys looked down the road to the south. Nothing was coming yet. But, they could all hear the distinct Chug – Chug – Chug.

Shortly, Harley said, "See that black smoke puffing up above the trees? It's over on the Sitka Road."

Louie and Les looked. They could see the smoke, and then they saw the stack of the tractor from which the smoke was puffing. Chills went up and down Louie's spine. Soon the threshing machine would arrive.

The boys ran to the road and sat next to a pine tree.

The exciting machine came down Eightieth Street. It rounded the corner on to their road. All the time the chugs got louder. The black smoke left a blue haze behind the tractor.

As Mr. Riggles approached the driveway of the Hooker farm, the boys ran beside him.

Dad directed Mr. Riggles through the barnyard gate just west of the barn.

He shouted to Mr. Riggles, "We want to make the straw pile just north of the calf shed."

Some men unhooked the threshing machine from the tractor. Then they unrolled a huge belt. The belt was very wide and long. They fastened one end of the belt to a pulley on the threshing machine. The other end was put on a pulley of the big smoky tractor. The belt was twisted halfway between the tractor and the threshing machine.

Some of the men were coming out of the wheat field with neatly loaded wagons filled with wheat bundles. They had pitched the bundles of wheat from the shocks on their wagons with pitchforks. Their horses stood quietly while they did this.

Soon, everything was ready and Dad shouted, "I think we're all ready, let's get rolling."

Mr. Riggles put the tractor in gear. The huge belt began to turn and whirr. The threshing machine hummed.

Harley, Louie and Les sat on the ground near the barn to watch. Dad had warned them to stay out of the way.

Mr. Hegan, a neighbor to the south of the Hooker farm, drove his horses and wagon near the threshing machine. He looked nervous. Sometimes the horses spooked from the noise of the machine. Mr. Hegan made certain that he had good control of the horses. They were driven right beside the threshing machine.

Then Mr. Hegan and another man forked bundles of wheat on to the table of the threshing machine. Dad had told Louie and his brothers beforehand that the table brought the wheat bundles to the separator of the machine. He said that inside the separator the grain was separated from the straw.

In a short time, straw was blowing out of a pipe at the back of the threshing machine. Louie thought the pipe from which the straw came looked like a dinosaur's neck.

The grain was flowing into a bin on the side of the threshing machine. Two men were letting the grain flow into large cloth bags from the bin.

Louie looked toward the wheat field across the road. He could see seven wagons being loaded with wheat bundles in the wheat field. Three of the wagons were being pulled by tractors. Four wagons had teams of horses pulling them. In 1942 farmers were just beginning to switch from horse power to tractor power. Louie's dad had both horses and a John Deere H Tractor.

Dad walked past the boys sitting near the barn. Louie shouted to Dad, "May I sit on the tractor with Mr. Riggles for awhile?"

Dad answered, "Yes, but be careful and don't get in the way."

Mr. Riggles smiled as Louie crawled up on the fender of the big tractor. Louie could see some oil spurting from the tractor as it chugged noisily.

Mr. Riggles and Louie didn't talk, because the tractor made too much noise for hearing.

Mr. Riggles was lame. Dad had told Louie and his brothers that Mr. Riggles had gotten a sickness when he was a very young boy. The sickness had paralyzed his legs, so he was not able to walk. He stayed on the tractor most of the day.

He started and stopped the big belt as was needed throughout the day.

Louie looked at Mr. Riggle's lame legs and thought, "My legs were like that last year, but now I'm walking."

Later that morning, Louie and his brothers went to where the straw was becoming a stack. It was already almost as tall as the calf shed. Louie and Les went close to where the straw was coming out of the pipe. Some of the blowing straw hit their bare feet.

Mr. Sneller, one of the men working, saw them and shouted, "Boys, get away! You may get buried under the straw."

This really scared them. So, they ran with Harley to the granary. The granary was upstairs in the tool shed. The granary stored the wheat, oats and barley for use during the winter.

Some men had the job of hauling big sacks of wheat from the threshing machine to the granary. This was hard work. The men had to climb up steps with a heavy bag of wheat on their shoulder. Louie noticed that the men's shirts were wet with sweat.

At noon Dad shouted to the men, "Dinner's ready, so we better stop to eat."

Mr. Riggles stopped the big belt that gave power to the threshing machine.

It seemed so quiet after the threshing machine and tractors were turned off. There was only the sound of an occasional whinny from a horse.

Two men carried Mr. Riggles to the house for dinner.

All the other men walked toward two laundry tubs placed on the grass under the willow trees. Mum and Virginia had filled them with water. The men took turns washing their dirty hands and faces. They used the laundry tubs as sinks.

Then the men went inside the big, white house. Some of the men sat around the big kitchen table. Others sat by smaller tables placed on the back porch.

Platters filled with crispy baked chicken and steamy bowls of mashed potatoes were setting on the tables. There also were bowls heaped with fresh green beans from the garden and plenty of canned applesauce for everyone. Pies were setting on the counter for dessert.

After Dad said a prayer, the men ate heartily the delicious meal that Mum and Virginia had prepared.

Harley, Louie, and Les sat at the dining room table. Marve ate with the men on the back porch.

Louie said to Harley and Les, "Boy, is this chicken good. I could eat chicken every day." Harley and Les were so busy eating, they didn't even respond.

After everyone had their fill, the men all went back to work again. Many bushels of grain were put in the granary.

At the supper table that night Dad said, "We sure had a good crop of wheat this year. We got over forty bushels to the acre. We should have plenty to feed the livestock throughout the winter."

Dad gave special thanks to God for the wonderful harvest of wheat. He also thanked God for the neighborhood men who helped reap the harvest.

Chapter

17

The Big Race

Summer had passed. The wheat and oat fields were harvested. Labor Day was celebrated.

Louie was worried about starting school the day after Labor Day. Would he get too tired? Would his burns bother him so he could not learn?

There was no kindergarten class at Brookside School, so Louie started school in the first grade. Of course, Louie could not have started the year before anyway – he was recovering from his burns.

It was the first day of school. Harley and Louie left for school at 8:00 A.M. Brookside School was over two miles away, and the boys had to walk. Marve and Virginia went to school in Fremont.

Louie's teacher was Mrs. Hile. She met all the students at the door and gave a pleasant greeting to each. Mrs. Hile told the first graders to sit at desks on the side of the room farthest from the windows. She placed the second graders at desks in the center of the room. The third graders were directed to the desks nearest the windows. The windows were high, so a student could not see out of them if they were sitting at their desk.

Louie saw a picture of George Washington and another one of Abraham Lincoln above the chalkboards in the front of the room. Mrs. Hile's desk was right in front of the chalkboards to one side of the room.

She called the classroom to order. There were fifteen students altogether in the first three grades at Brookside School. There were eighteen students in the room just past the sliding wooden doors. Harley, who was in the fourth grade, was in that room.

During recess that morning, Louie played with Curt, who was also a first grader. Curt lived East of Brookside School, past Brooks Creek.

Curt ran from the red brick schoolhouse toward the fence on the other side of the playground. He yelled, "Come on, Louie, race me to the fence."

Louie followed, but he couldn't keep up. His legs were stiff, and his burns ached. Curt was waiting at the fence. Louie was scratching his legs when he arrived. His burns always itched when he ran.

In the days that followed, Louie enjoyed learning how to read. It was fun to learn about new places in the world. He thought reading about a place near the Atlantic Ocean called Gloucester was especially exciting. There was a picture in one book of fishing boats coming in the harbor with fish in boxes that had been caught in nets.

Often Louie had to walk home from school alone. Sometimes in the fall, Louie picked apples from trees near the road. One time he picked a crabapple from a tree near Sneller's farm. It was sour, and he spit it out.

Harley's class was excused over an hour later than Louie's. Louie was home before Harley got out of school.

Louie was afraid of strange dogs. When a dog came barking from behind a farmhouse, he would cringe in fear. He soon learned which houses had barking dogs. To escape from them, he walked far out in the field across from those farm houses so the dogs wouldn't see him.

One morning, the mothers of Louie's class were invited to school. His class presented a play on being a good patriot of our country.

Mrs. Pall, one of the mothers, asked Mum why Louie always walked out in her field instead of down the road. Louie overheard her ask the question.

Mum looked at him and asked, "Why don't you stay on the road when you're walking home from school?" Immediately Mum could see there were tears in his eyes.

Louie blurted out, "I'm scared of some people's dogs. They always bark at me."

Mum comforted Louie and told him that he could go home at noon with her for that day. At least he didn't have to face the dogs that day.

From that day on, he took every opportunity to wait until the older kids got excused. That way he had Harley and others to walk with him past the scary dogs.

One sunny winter day as Louie was walking home alone, he noticed a snow plow coming down the road. He could see the snow flying in front of the plow. Louie ran to the opposite side of the road. He ran over the bank and through the ditch. However, he stayed near the road. Louie wanted the snow to fly on him as the plow passed.

The snow plow man slowed down – he stopped right in front of Louie. Louie wondered if the snow plow man was going to give him a ride home.

The man rolled down his window on his truck. He looked sternly at Louie and said, "Little boy, you must not get in the path of flying snow. The plow might pick up a stone or piece of hard ice. You may get hit in the head and get injured."

Louie was shaking with fear. He didn't know what to say. He nodded in agreement and finally blurted out, "Okay!"

Then the snow plow man rolled his window up and moved on down the road. Louie watched the snow fly, but he didn't see any rocks or chunks of ice. However, you can be sure that he never tried that again.

As the school year progressed, Louie's legs got stronger. He often played running games with the other children at school.

One game he played was "Eenee Inee Over". The game was played by the pump house. The pump house stored the pump that provided water for the school.

For the game, a team was on each side of the building. One team threw a tennis ball over the roof. They would yell "Eenee Inee Over" when they threw it over. The other team tried to catch the ball before it hit the ground. If someone did catch the ball, they ran around the building and tried to hit the other team's players before they could get to the opposite side. If someone got hit, they joined the other team. The game was over when all the players were on one team.

Other games that Louie played at recess were "Pom Pom Pull Away" and "Cops and Robbers." Recess was a fun time.

Once in the spring of that school year, Louie stayed later, so he could walk home with Harley. On the way home they stopped at Spring Creek to play. Spring Creek crossed the road west of Brookside School. The boys looked for crabs and frogs in the creek.

Harley yelled, "Louie, come and look at the big crab under this log."

Louie ran through the ditch and down a small hill. His legs stretched too far, and he stumbled and hurt his burns. He lay on the ground and groaned.

Harley shouted, "What happened?"

"I hurt my burns," responded Louie.

Harley helped him stand up. He was bleeding, but with Harley's help was able to limp home.

When they came through the door of the big, white house, Mum could see there was something wrong. She asked him, "What's wrong with you?"

"I stumbled and fell at Spring Creek," he answered. "I hurt my burns!"

Mum examined the sore and put a bandage on it.

During the month of May at school, the boys and girls were allowed to eat their lunches outside on warm, sunny days. Dandelions were appearing in the grass. Some of the boys even took their shoes off and went barefoot.

Herm often played with Louie during the noon recess. He lived south of Brookside School.

One day Herm said to Louie, "Mrs. Hile has contests for each grade on the last day of school. Usually she has us race."

"Oh!" thought Louie, "I wonder if my legs are strong and fast enough to win a race?" Louie knew that Curt would be hard to beat.

After that on his lonely walks home from school, Louie practiced running. He would run the distance of three telephone poles. Then he would walk two. The telephone poles were located along side of the road. There were wires stretched between them. By running and walking in this way, Louie could run and then rest. He could get stronger for the race on the last day of school.

The final day of school arrived. It was the Friday before Memorial Day. Harley and Louie started for school early that day.

When they reached school, all the boys and girls were chattering about the contests that they knew were coming. They also were glad that this was the last day of school before the long summer vacation.

After a short time in school, Mrs. Hile announced, "Boys and girls, it's time to go outside for some fun and contests." Louie's heart began beating fast with anticipation.

Since the first grade was the youngest class, Mrs. Hile called them first to her side. She told them that they would race from the fence to the ball diamond.

Louie looked at Curt. Curt had long legs and could take bigger steps. But, Louie was determined to try his best to win.

Mrs. Hile told the first graders to line up at the fence. There were five altogether, three boys and two girls. Curt lined up beside Louie.

Louie's face was flushed. He was nervous.

Mrs. Hile stood by the ball diamond to see who won. She shouted, "Everyone ready?" Then she yelled, "On your marks – Get set – Go!"

Curt sprinted out ahead of Louie and the others. Louie dug his feet in the grass with every step. He edged closer to Curt. He could hear Curt grunting with every step. Louie passed him. The children watching the race were screaming!

Then Curt gave a burst of speed and came right even with him. Louie looked ahead and saw Mrs. Hile standing at the finish line.

Did he have enough strength to finish the race? His legs ached. He gritted his teeth, and inched slowly ahead of Curt.

In a moment the race was over. Louie won the race by inches.

Mrs. Hile congratulated him and gave him a pencil for winning. The yellow pencil had printed on one side, Brookside Standard School. Louie decided that he would save the pencil for the next year of school, when he was in the second grade.

That night as Louie lay in bed, before he fell asleep, he had a happy heart. A whole summer of fun and interesting events on the Hooker farm lay ahead. He was comfortable in his bed upstairs in the big, white farm house south of Reeman. Not only had he won a race at school, but his burns were healed and he was well again.

WHEN EVENTS HAPPENED ON THE
HOOKER FARM IN EARLY 1940s

JANUARY
The garden seeds are ordered from a seed catalog.

FEBRUARY
Hogs are butchered and prepared for eating.
Preparation is made for baby chicks.

MARCH
Maple sap is harvested.
Baby chicks arrive from the hatchery.

APRIL
The lawn is raked, and the yard is made tidy and neat.
Oats and peas are planted in fields.
The last of the corn stalks are brought from stacks to
the barn and fed to the cattle.

MAY
Field corn is planted.
The garden seeds are planted in the garden.

JUNE
Hay is harvested – It was not baled, but put loose in
the barn.

JULY
Peas are harvested for Gerbers to make baby food.

Winter wheat is cut by binder late in the month and put in shocks.
Wheat is threshed within two weeks of cutting.

AUGUST
The hay is harvested for a second time. The second cutting is much smaller than the first cutting.
The chicks that arrived in March start laying eggs.

SEPTEMBER
Winter wheat is planted after Sept. 15. This wheat is harvested the next July.
Corn is cut and put in shocks toward end of month. Early frost sometimes makes this happen sooner.

OCTOBER
Corn is husked. The corn ears are separated from the stalks by hand. The ears are put in the corn crib, and the stalks are put in a stack.
Potatoes are dug and stored in the basement.
Walnuts and hickory nuts are picked up and stored.

NOVEMBER
Farm tools and machinery are cleaned and put away in the shed for winter.

DECEMBER
Cattle are snug in the barn for the winter.
Christmas tree is cut and decorated.